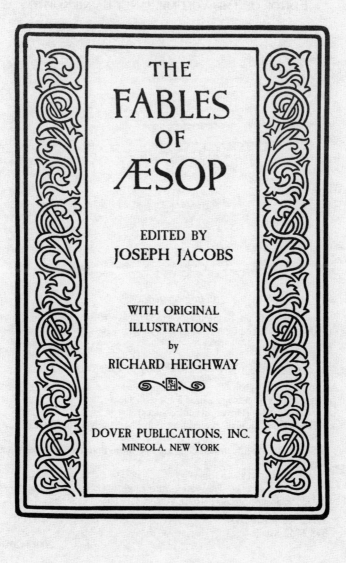

THE
FABLES
OF
ÆSOP

EDITED BY
JOSEPH JACOBS

WITH ORIGINAL
ILLUSTRATIONS
by
RICHARD HEIGHWAY

DOVER PUBLICATIONS, INC.
MINEOLA, NEW YORK

EDITOR OF THIS VOLUME: JANET BAINE KOPITO

Bibliographical Note

This Dover edition, first published in 2002, is a revised republication of the edition published by Macmillan, London, in 1894.

Library of Congress Cataloging-in-Publication Data

Aesop's fables. English.
   The fables of Aesop / edited by Joseph Jacobs.
       p. cm. — (Dover juvenile classics)
   Rev. publication of the edition published by Macmillan, London, 1894.
   Summary: An illustrated collection of more than eighty fables from Aesop.
   ISBN 0-486-41859-6 (pbk.)
   1. Fables, Greek—Translation into English. [1. Fables. 2. Folklore.] I. Jacobs, Joseph, 1854–1916. II. Aesop. III. Title. IV. Series.

PZ8.2.A254 Fab 2001
398.24′52—dc21

                                                                    2001042086

Manufactured in the United States of America
Dover Publications, Inc., 31 East 2nd Street, Mineola, N.Y. 11501

LIST OF FABLES

THE
FABLES
OF
ÆSOP

The·Cock·and·the·Pearl·

A COCK was once strutting up and down the farmyard among the hens when suddenly he espied something shining amid the straw. "Ho! ho!" quoth he, "that's for me," and soon rooted it out from beneath the straw. What did it turn out to be but a Pearl that by some chance had been lost in the yard? "You may be a treasure," quoth Master Cock, "to men that prize you, but for me I would rather have a single barley-corn than a peck of pearls.

Precious things are for those that can prize them."

"Ho! ho!" quoth he, "that's for me."

THE · WOLF · AND · THE · LAMB ·

ONCE upon a time a Wolf was lap-
ping at a spring on a hillside,
when, looking up, what should he
see but a Lamb just beginning
to drink a little lower down. "There's my
supper," thought he, "if only I can find some
excuse to seize it." Then he called out to the
Lamb, "How dare you muddle the water from
which I am drinking?"

"Nay, master, nay," said Lambikin; "if
the water be muddy up there, I cannot be the
cause of it, for it runs down from you to me.

"Well, then," said the Wolf, "why did you call me bad names this time last year?"

"That cannot be," said the Lamb : "I am only six months old."

"I don't care," snarled the Wolf; "if it was not you, it was your father;" and with that he rushed upon the poor little Lamb and—

Warra warra warra warra warra—

ate her all up.   But before she died she gasped out—

"Any excuse will serve a tyrant."

The Dog & the Shadow.

IT happened that a Dog had got a piece of meat and was carrying it home in his mouth to eat it in peace. Now on his way home he had to cross a plank lying across a running brook. As he crossed, he looked down and saw his own shadow reflected in the water beneath. Thinking it was another dog with another piece of meat, he made up his mind to have that also. So he made a snap at the shadow in the water, but as he opened his mouth the piece of meat fell out, dropped into the water and was never seen more.

Beware lest you lose the substance by grasping at the shadow.

The Lion's Share

THE Lion went once a-hunting along with the Fox, the Jackal, and the Wolf. They hunted and they hunted till at last they surprised a Stag, and soon took its life. Then came the question how the spoil should be divided. "Quarter me this Stag," roared the Lion; so the other animals skinned it and cut it into four parts. Then the Lion took his stand in front of the carcass and pronounced judgment: "The first quarter is for me in my capacity as King of Beasts; the second is mine as arbiter; another share comes to me for my part in the chase; and as for the fourth quarter, well, as for that, I should like to see which of you will dare to lay a paw upon it."

"Humph," grumbled the Fox as he walked away with his tail between his legs; but he spoke in a low growl—

"𝔜ou may share the labours of the great, but you will not share the spoil."

·The·Wolf·and·the·Crane·

A WOLF had been gorging on an animal he had killed, when suddenly a small bone in the meat stuck in his throat and he could not swallow it. He soon felt terrible pain in his throat, and ran up and down groaning and groaning and seeking for something to relieve the pain. He tried to induce every one he met to remove the bone. "I would give anything," said he, "if you would take it out." At last the Crane agreed to try, and told the Wolf to lie on his side and open his jaws as wide as he could. Then the Crane put its long neck down the Wolf's throat, and with its beak loosened the bone, till at last it got it out.

"Will you kindly give me the reward you promised?" said the Crane.

The Wolf grinned and showed his teeth and said: "Be content. You have put your head inside a Wolf's mouth and taken it out again in safety; that ought to be reward enough for you."

𝔊ratitude and greed go not together.

The Man and the Serpent.

COUNTRYMAN'S son by accident trod upon a Serpent's tail, which turned and bit him so that he died. The father in a rage got his axe, and pursuing the Serpent, cut off part of its tail. So the Serpent in revenge began stinging several of the Farmer's cattle and caused him severe loss. Well, the Farmer thought it best to make it up with the Serpent, and brought food and honey to the mouth of its lair, and said to it : "Let's forget and forgive ; perhaps you were right to punish my son, and take vengeance on my cattle, but surely I was right in trying to revenge him; now that we are both satisfied why should not we be friends again?"

"No, no," said the Serpent; "take away your gifts; you can never forget the death of your son, nor I the loss of my tail."

Injuries may be forgiven, but not forgotten.

The Town Mouse
& the Country Mouse.

NOW you must know that a Town Mouse once upon a time went on a visit to his cousin in the country. He was rough and ready, this cousin, but he loved his town friend and made him heartily welcome. Beans and bacon, cheese and bread, were all he had to offer, but he offered them freely. The Town Mouse rather turned up his

long nose at this country fare, and said : "I cannot
understand, Cousin, how you can put up with
such poor food as this, but of course you cannot
expect anything better in the country ; come
you with me and I will show you how to live.
When you have been in town a week you will
wonder how you could ever have stood a country
life."   No sooner said than done : the two mice
set off for the town and arrived at the Town
Mouse's residence late at night.   "You will
want some refreshment after our long journey,"
said the polite Town Mouse, and took his friend
into the grand dining-room.   There they
found the remains of a fine feast, and soon the
two mice were eating up jellies and cakes and
all that was nice.   Suddenly they heard growl-
ing and barking.   "What is that?" said the
Country Mouse.   "It is only the dogs of the
house," answered the other.   "Only!" said the
Country Mouse.   "I do not like that music at

my dinner." Just at that moment the door
flew open, in came two huge mastiffs, and the
two mice had to scamper down and run off.
"Good-bye, Cousin," said the Country Mouse.
"What! going so soon?" said the other.
"Yes," he replied ;

"Better beans and bacon in peace than cakes
and ale in fear."

THE FOX & THE CROW

A FOX once saw a Crow fly off with a piece of cheese in its beak and settle on a branch of a tree. "That's for me, as I am a Fox," said Master Renard, and he walked up to the foot of the tree. "Good-day, Mistress Crow," he cried. "How well you are looking to-day : how glossy your feathers ; how bright your eye. I feel sure your voice must surpass that of other birds, just as your figure does ; let me hear but one song from you that I may greet you as the Queen of Birds." The 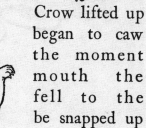 Crow lifted up her head and began to caw her best, but the moment she opened her mouth the piece of cheese fell to the ground, only to be snapped up

by Master Fox. "That will do," said he.
"That was all I wanted. In exchange for
your cheese I will give you a piece of advice
for the future—

Do not trust flatterers."

The Flatterer doth rob by stealth,
his victim, both of Wit and Wealth.

THE SICK LION

A LION had come to the end of his days and lay sick unto death at the mouth of his cave, gasping for breath. The animals, his subjects, came round him and drew nearer as he grew more and more helpless. When they saw him on the point of death they thought to themselves: "Now is the time to pay off old grudges." So the Boar came up and drove at him with his tusks; then a Bull gored him with his horns; still the Lion lay helpless before them: so the Ass, feeling quite safe from danger, came up, and turning his tail to the old Lion kicked up his heels into his face. "This is a double death," growled the Lion.

"Only cowards insult dying Majesty."

THE ASS
AND
THE LAP-DOG

A FARMER one day came to the stables to see to his beasts of burden : among them was his favourite Ass, that was always well fed and often carried his master. With the Farmer came his Lapdog, who danced about and licked his hand and frisked about as happy as could be. The Farmer felt in his pocket, gave the Lapdog some dainty food, and sat down while he gave his orders to his servants. The Lapdog jumped into his master's lap, and lay there blinking while the Farmer stroked his ears. The Ass, seeing this, broke loose from his halter and commenced prancing about in imitation of the Lapdog. The Farmer could not hold his sides with laughter, so the Ass went up to him, and putting his feet upon the Farmer's shoulder attempted to climb into his lap. The Farmer's servants rushed up with sticks and pitchforks and soon taught the ass that

Clumsy jesting is no joke.

Once when a Lion was
asleep a little Mouse began
running up and down upon
him; this soon wakened
the Lion, who placed his
huge paw upon him, and opened his big jaws

to swallow him. "Pardon, O King," cried
the little Mouse; "forgive me this time, I
shall never forget it : who knows but what
I may be able to do you a turn some of these
days?" The Lion was so tickled at the idea
of the Mouse being able to help him, that he
lifted up his paw and let him go. Some time
after the Lion was caught in a trap, and the
hunters, who desired to carry him alive to the
King, tied him to a tree while they went in
search of a waggon to carry him on. Just
then the little Mouse happened to pass by,
and seeing the sad plight in which the Lion
was, went up to him and soon gnawed away
the ropes that bound the King of the Beasts.
"Was I not right?" said the little Mouse.

Little friends
may prove
great
friends

THE = SWALLOW = AND THE = OTHER = BIRDS =

IT happened that a Countryman was sowing some hemp seeds in a field where a Swallow and some other birds were hopping about picking up their food. "Beware of that man," quoth the Swallow. "Why, what is he doing?" said the others. "That is hemp seed he is sowing; be careful to pick up every one of the seeds, or else you will repent it." The birds paid no heed to the Swallow's words, and by and by the hemp grew up and was made into cord, and of the cords nets were made, and many a bird that had despised the

Swallow's advice was caught in nets made out of that very hemp. "What did I tell you?" said the Swallow.

"Destroy the seed of evil, or it will grow up to your ruin."

THE FROGS
desiring
a KING

The FROGS DESIRING A KING

Frogs were living as happy as could be in a marshy swamp that just suited them; they went splashing about caring for nobody and nobody troubling with them. But some of them thought that this was not right, that they should have a king and a proper constitution, so they determined to send up a petition to Jove to give them what they wanted. "Mighty Jove," they cried, "send unto us a king that will rule over us and keep us in order." Jove laughed at their croaking, and threw down into the swamp a huge Log, which came down—*kerplash*—into the swamp. The Frogs were frightened out of their lives by the commotion made in their midst, and all rushed to the bank to look at the horrible monster; but after a time, seeing

that it did not move, one or two of the boldest
of them ventured out towards the Log, and
even dared to touch it ; still it did not move.
Then the greatest hero of the Frogs jumped
upon the Log and commenced dancing up
and down upon it, thereupon all the Frogs
came and did the same ; and for some time
the Frogs went about their business every day
without taking the slightest notice of their
new King Log lying in their midst.   But
this did not suit them, so they sent another
petition to Jove, and said to him : " We want
a real king ; one that will really rule over
us."   Now this made Jove
angry, so he sent among them
a big Stork that soon set
to work gobbling them all
up.   Then the Frogs repented
when too late.

Better no rule
than cruel rule.

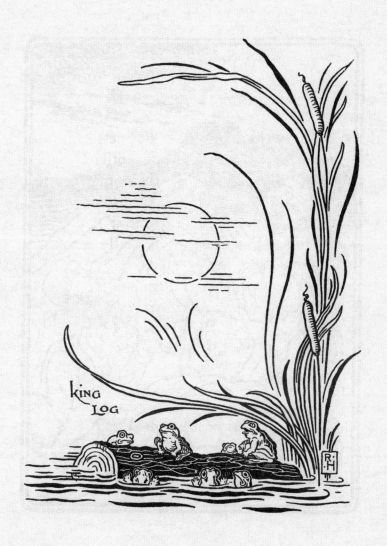

KING
LOG

THE MOUNTAINS IN LABOUR

ONE day the Countrymen noticed that the Mountains were in labour; smoke came out of their summits, the earth was quaking at their feet, trees were crashing, and huge rocks were tumbling. They felt sure that something horrible was going to happen. They all gathered together in one place to see what terrible thing this would be. They waited

and they waited, but nothing came. At last
there was a still more violent earthquake, and
a huge gap appeared in the side of the Mountains. They all fell down upon their knees
and waited. At last, and at last, a teeny, tiny
mouse poked its little head and bristles out
of the gap and came running down towards
them ; and ever after they used to say :

"𝔐uch outcry, little outcome."

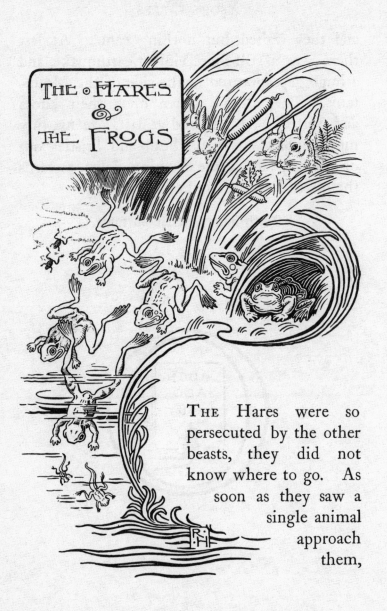

THE Hares were so persecuted by the other beasts, they did not know where to go. As soon as they saw a single animal approach them,

off they used to run.   One day they saw
a troop of wild Horses stampeding about,
and in quite a panic all the Hares scuttled off
to a lake hard by, determined to drown themselves rather than live in such a continual
state of fear.   But just as they got near the
bank of the lake, a troop of Frogs, frightened
in their turn by the approach of the Hares,
scuttled off, and jumped into the water.
"Truly," said one of the Hares, "things are
not so bad as they seem :

𝔗here is always some one worse off
than yourself."

THE·WOLF·&·THE·KID·

 KID was perched up on the top of a house, and looking down saw a Wolf passing under him. Immediately he began to revile and attack his enemy. "Murderer and thief," he cried, "what do you here near honest folks' houses? How dare you make an appearance where your vile deeds are known?"

"Curse away, my young friend," said the Wolf.

"It is easy to be brave from a safe distance."

"It is easy to be brave from a safe distance."

THE WOODMAN AND THE SERPENT.

ONE wintry day a Woodman was tramping home from his work when he saw something black lying on the snow. When he came closer, he saw it was a Serpent to all appearance dead. But he took it up and put it in his bosom to warm while he hurried home. As soon as he got indoors he put the Serpent down on the hearth before the fire. The children watched it and saw it slowly come to life again. Then one of them stooped down to stroke it, but the Serpent raised its head and put out its fangs and was about to sting the child to death. So the Woodman seized his axe, and with one stroke cut the Serpent in two. "Ah," said he,

"𝕹𝖔 𝖌𝖗𝖆𝖙𝖎𝖙𝖚𝖉𝖊 𝖋𝖗𝖔𝖒 𝖙𝖍𝖊 𝖜𝖎𝖈𝖐𝖊𝖉."

The Woodman and
the Serpent

THE BALD ~MAN & THE FLY.

THE BALD MAN & THE FLY.

THERE was once a Bald Man who sat down after work on a hot summer's day. A Fly came up and kept buzzing about his bald pate, and stinging him from time to time. The Man aimed a blow at his little enemy, but—*whack*—his palm came on his head instead; again the Fly tormented him, but this time the Man was wiser and said:

"You will only injure yourself if you take notice of despicable enemies."

The Fox & the Stork

AT one time the Fox and the Stork were on visiting terms and seemed very good friends. So the Fox invited the Stork to dinner, and for a joke put nothing before her but some soup in a very shallow dish. This the Fox could easily lap up, but the Stork could only wet the end of her long bill in it, and left the meal as hungry as when she began. "I am sorry," said the Fox, "the soup is not to your liking."

"Pray do not apologise," said the Stork.
"I hope you will return this visit, and come
and dine with me soon." So a day was
appointed when the Fox should visit the
Stork ; but when they were seated at table all
that was for their dinner was contained in
a very long-necked jar with a narrow
mouth, in which the Fox
could not insert his snout,
so all he could manage to
do was to lick the outside
of the jar.

"I will not apologise for
the dinner," said the Stork :

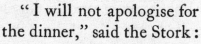

"One bad turn
deserves another."

The Fox
and the Mask

A FOX had by some means got into the store-room of a theatre. Suddenly he observed a face glaring down on him, and began to be very frightened ; but looking more closely he found it was only a Mask, such as actors use to put over their face. "Ah," said the Fox, "you look very fine ; it is a pity you have not got any brains."

Outside show is a poor substitute for inner worth.

THE JAY & THE PEACOCK

A Jay venturing into a yard where Peacocks used to walk, found there a number of feathers which had fallen from the Peacocks when they were moulting. He tied them all to his tail and strutted down towards the Peacocks. When he came near them they soon discovered the cheat, and striding up to him pecked at him and plucked away his borrowed plumes. So the Jay could do no better than go back to the other Jays, who had watched his behaviour from a distance ; but they were equally annoyed with him, and told him

"It is not only fine feathers that make fine birds."

THE FROG AND THE OX

"OH FATHER," said a little Frog to the big one sitting by the side of a pool, "I have seen such a terrible monster! It was as big as a mountain, with horns on its head, and a long tail, and it had hoofs divided in two."

"Tush, child, tush," said the old Frog, "that was only Farmer White's Ox. It isn't so big either; he may be a little bit taller than I, but I could easily make myself quite as broad; just you see." So he blew himself out, and blew himself out, and blew himself out. "Was he as big as that?" asked he.

"Oh, much bigger than that," said the young Frog.

Again the old one blew himself out, and asked the young one if the Ox was as big as that.

"Bigger, father, bigger," was the reply.

So the Frog took a deep breath, and blew and blew and blew, and swelled and swelled and swelled. And then he said: "I'm sure the Ox is not as big as ——" But at this moment he burst.

Self=conceit may lead to self=destruction.

ANDROCLES

A SLAVE named Androcles once escaped from his master and fled to the forest. As he was wandering about there he came upon a Lion lying down moaning and groaning. At first he turned to flee, but finding that the Lion did not pursue him, he turned back and went up to him. As he came near, the Lion put out his paw, which was all swollen and bleeding, and Androcles found that a huge thorn had got into it, and was causing all the pain. He pulled out the thorn and bound up the paw of the Lion, who was soon able to rise and lick the hand of Androcles like a dog. Then the Lion took Androcles to his cave, and every day used to bring him meat from which to live. But shortly afterwards both Androcles and the Lion were captured, and the slave was sentenced to be thrown to the

Lion, after the latter had been kept without food for several days. The Emperor and all his Court came to see the spectacle, and Androcles was led out into the middle of the arena. Soon the Lion was let loose from his den, and rushed bounding and roaring towards his victim. But as soon as he came near to Androcles he recognised his friend, and fawned upon him, and licked his hands like a friendly dog. The Emperor, surprised at this, summoned Androcles to him, who told him the whole story. Whereupon the slave was pardoned and freed, and the Lion let loose to his native forest.

Gratitude is the sign of noble souls.

The Bat the Birds & the Beasts.

A GREAT conflict was about to come off between the Birds and the Beasts. When the two armies were collected together the Bat hesitated which to join. The Birds that passed his perch said : "Come with us"; but he said : "I am a Beast." Later on, some Beasts who were passing underneath him looked up and said : "Come with us"; but he said : "I am a Bird." Luckily at the last moment peace was made, and no battle took place, so the Bat came to the Birds and wished to join in the rejoicings, but they all turned against him and he had to fly away.

He then went to the Beasts, but had soon to
beat a retreat, or else they would have torn
him to pieces. "Ah," said the Bat, "I see
now

𝔥𝔢 that is neither one thing nor the
other has no friends."

The Hart and the Hunter.

THE Hart was once drinking from a pool and admiring the noble figure he made there. "Ah," said he, "where can you see such noble horns as these, with such antlers! I wish I had legs more worthy to bear such a noble crown; it is a pity they are so slim and slight." At that moment a Hunter approached and sent an arrow whistling after him. Away bounded the Hart, and soon, by the aid of his nimble legs, was nearly out of sight of the Hunter; but not noticing where he was going, he passed under some trees with branches growing low down in which his antlers were caught, so that the Hunter had time to come up. "Alas! alas!" cried the Hart:

"We often despise what is most useful
to us."

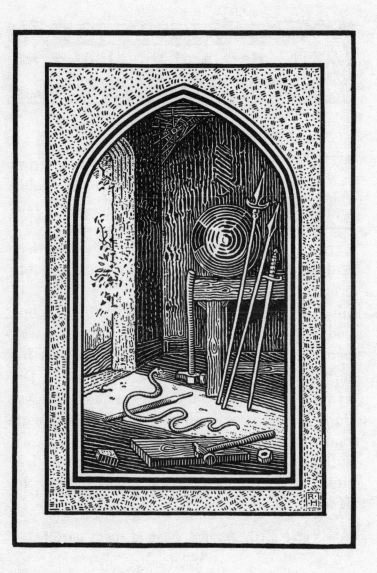

The Serpent & the File.

A Serpent in the course of its wanderings came into an armourer's shop. As he glided over the floor he felt his skin pricked by a file lying there. In a rage he turned round upon it and tried to dart his fangs into it; but he could do no harm to heavy iron and had soon to give over his wrath.

It is useless attacking the insensible.

THE MAN AND THE WOOD

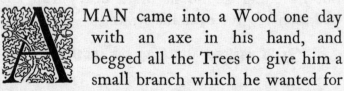MAN came into a Wood one day with an axe in his hand, and begged all the Trees to give him a small branch which he wanted for a particular purpose. The Trees were good-natured and gave him one of their branches. What did the Man do but fix it into the axe-head, and soon set to work cutting down tree

after tree. Then the Trees saw how foolish they had been in giving their enemy the means of destroying themselves.

The · Dog · and the · Wolf · ◦◦

A GAUNT Wolf was almost dead with hunger when he happened to meet a House-dog who was passing by. "Ah, Cousin," said the Dog, "I knew how it would be ; your irregular life will soon be the ruin of you. Why do you not work steadily as I do, and get your food regularly given to you?"

"I would have no objection," said the Wolf, "if I could only get a place."

"I will easily arrange that for you," said the Dog; "come with me to my master and you shall share my work."

So the Wolf and the Dog went towards the town together. On the way there the Wolf noticed that the hair on a certain part of the Dog's neck was very much worn away, so he asked him how that had come about.

"Oh, it is nothing," said the Dog.   "That is only the place where the collar is put on at night to keep me chained up ; it chafes a bit, but one soon gets used to it."

"Is that all?" said the Wolf.   "Then good-bye to you, Master Dog.

"Better starve free than be a fat slave."

The Belly & the Members

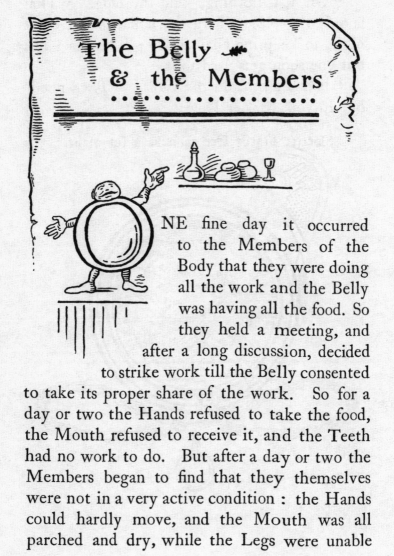

ONE fine day it occurred to the Members of the Body that they were doing all the work and the Belly was having all the food. So they held a meeting, and after a long discussion, decided to strike work till the Belly consented to take its proper share of the work. So for a day or two the Hands refused to take the food, the Mouth refused to receive it, and the Teeth had no work to do. But after a day or two the Members began to find that they themselves were not in a very active condition : the Hands could hardly move, and the Mouth was all parched and dry, while the Legs were unable to support the rest. So thus they found that even the Belly in its dull quiet way was doing necessary work for the Body, and that all must work together or the Body will go to pieces.

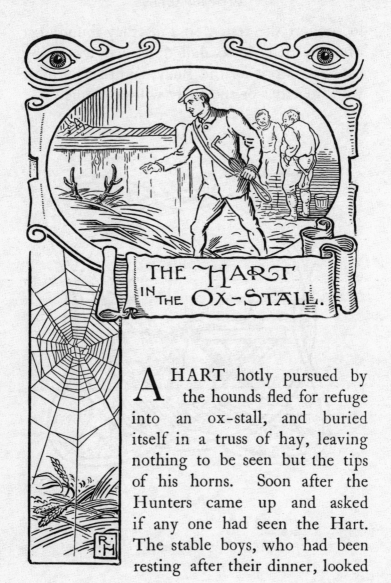

THE HART IN THE OX-STALL.

A HART hotly pursued by the hounds fled for refuge into an ox-stall, and buried itself in a truss of hay, leaving nothing to be seen but the tips of his horns. Soon after the Hunters came up and asked if any one had seen the Hart. The stable boys, who had been resting after their dinner, looked round, but could see nothing, and the Hunters went away. Shortly afterwards the master came in, and, looking round, saw that something unusual had taken place. He pointed to the truss of hay and said: "What are those two curious things sticking out of the hay?" And when the stable boys came to look they discovered the Hart, and soon made an end of him. He thus learnt that

𝕹𝖔𝖙𝖍𝖎𝖓𝖌 𝖊𝖘𝖈𝖆𝖕𝖊𝖘 𝖙𝖍𝖊 𝖒𝖆𝖘𝖙𝖊𝖗'𝖘 𝖊𝖞𝖊.

THE FOX & THE GRAPES

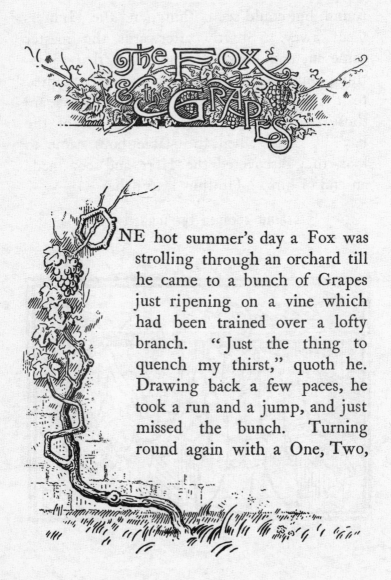

ONE hot summer's day a Fox was strolling through an orchard till he came to a bunch of Grapes just ripening on a vine which had been trained over a lofty branch. "Just the thing to quench my thirst," quoth he. Drawing back a few paces, he took a run and a jump, and just missed the bunch. Turning round again with a One, Two,

Three, he jumped up, but with no greater success. Again and again he tried after the tempting morsel, but at last had to give it up, and walked away with his nose in the air, saying : "I am sure they are sour."

𝔍𝔱 𝔦𝔰 𝔢𝔞𝔰𝔶 𝔱𝔬 𝔡𝔢𝔰𝔭𝔦𝔰𝔢 𝔴𝔥𝔞𝔱 𝔶𝔬𝔲 𝔠𝔞𝔫𝔫𝔬𝔱 𝔤𝔢𝔱.

THE
PEACOCK
& JUNO:

THE PEACOCK & JUNO

 PEACOCK once placed a petition before Juno desiring to have the voice of a nightingale in addition to his other attractions ; but Juno refused his request. When he persisted, and pointed out that he was her favourite bird, she said :

"𝔅e content with your lot; one cannot be first in everything."

⊙THE⊙HORSE⊙HUNTER⊙&⊙STAG⊙

A QUARREL had arisen between the Horse and the Stag, so the Horse came to a Hunter to ask his help to take revenge on the Stag. The Hunter agreed, but said : "If you desire to conquer the Stag, you must permit me to place this piece of iron between your jaws, so that I may guide you with these reins, and allow this saddle to be placed upon your back so that I may keep steady upon you as we follow after the enemy." The Horse agreed to the conditions, and the Hunter soon saddled and bridled him. Then with the aid of the Hunter the Horse soon overcame the Stag, and said to the Hunter : "Now, get off, and remove those things from my mouth and back."

"Not so fast, friend," said the Hunter. "I have now got you under bit and spur, and prefer to keep you as you are at present."

If you allow men to use you for your own purposes, they will use you for theirs.

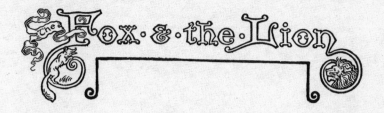

The Fox & the Lion

WHEN first the Fox saw the Lion he was terribly frightened, and ran away and hid himself in the wood. Next time however he came near the King of Beasts he stopped at a safe distance and watched him pass by. The third time they came near one another the Fox went straight up to the Lion and passed the time of day with him, asking him how his family were, and when he should have the pleasure of seeing him again ; then turning his tail, he parted from the Lion without much ceremony.

Familiarity breeds contempt.

THE LION & THE STATUE

A MAN and a Lion were discussing the relative strength of men and lions in general. The Man contended that he and his fellows were stronger than lions by reason of their greater intelligence. "Come now with me," he cried, "and I will soon prove that I am right." So he took him into the public gardens and showed him a statue of Hercules overcoming the Lion and tearing his mouth in two.

"That is all very well," said the Lion, "but proves nothing, for it was a man who made the statue."

We can easily represent things as we wish them to be.

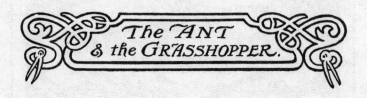

The ANT & the GRASSHOPPER.

IN a field one summer's day a Grasshopper was hopping about, chirping and singing to its heart's content. An Ant passed by, bearing along with great toil an ear of corn he was taking to the nest.

"Why not come and chat with me," said the Grasshopper, "instead of toiling and moiling in that way?"

"I am helping to lay up food for the winter," said the Ant, "and recommend you to do the same."

"Why bother about winter?" said the Grasshopper; "we have got plenty of food at present.' But the Ant went on its way and continued its toil.   When the winter came the Grasshopper had no food, and found itself dying of hunger, while it saw the ants distributing every day corn and grain from the stores they had collected in the summer.   Then the Grasshopper knew

𝕴𝖙 𝖎𝖘 𝖇𝖊𝖘𝖙 𝖙𝖔 𝖕𝖗𝖊𝖕𝖆𝖗𝖊 𝖋𝖔𝖗 𝖙𝖍𝖊 𝖉𝖆𝖞𝖘 𝖔𝖋 𝖓𝖊𝖈𝖊𝖘𝖘𝖎𝖙𝖞.

THE TREE AND THE REED

"WELL, little one," said a Tree to a Reed that was growing at its foot, "why do you not plant your feet deeply in the ground, and raise your head boldly in the air as I do?"

"I am contented with my lot," said the Reed. "I may not be so grand, but I think I am safer."

"Safe!" sneered the Tree. "Who shall pluck me up by the roots or bow my head to the ground?" But it soon had to repent of its boasting, for a hurricane arose which tore it up from its roots, and cast it a useless log on the ground, while the little Reed, bending to the force of the wind, soon stood upright again when the storm had passed over.

Obscurity often brings safety.

The Fox & the Cat.

A FOX was boasting to a Cat of its clever devices for escaping its enemies. "I have a whole bag of tricks," he said, "which contains a hundred ways of escaping my enemies."

"I have only one," said the Cat; "but I can generally manage with that." Just at that moment they heard the cry of a pack of hounds coming towards them, and the Cat immediately scampered up a tree and hid herself in the boughs. "This is my plan," said the Cat. "What are you going to do?" The Fox thought first of one way, then of another, and while he was debating the hounds came nearer and nearer, and at last the Fox in his confusion was caught up by the hounds

and soon killed by the huntsmen.   Miss Puss,
who had been looking on, said :

"𝔅etter one safe way than a hundred on
which you cannot reckon."

THE WOLF IN · SHEEP'S · CLOTHING ·

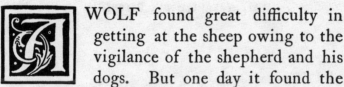

WOLF found great difficulty in getting at the sheep owing to the vigilance of the shepherd and his dogs. But one day it found the skin of a sheep that had been flayed and thrown aside, so it put it on over its own pelt and strolled down among the sheep. The Lamb that belonged to the sheep, whose

skin the Wolf was wearing, began to follow
the Wolf in the Sheep's clothing; so, leading
the Lamb a little apart, he soon made a meal
off her, and for some time he succeeded in
deceiving the sheep, and enjoying hearty
meals.

Appearances are deceptive.

The Dog in the Manger.

A DOG looking out for its afternoon nap jumped into the Manger of an Ox and lay there cosily upon the straw. But soon the Ox, returning from its afternoon work, came up to the Manger and wanted to eat some of the straw. The Dog in a rage, being awakened from its slumber, stood up and barked at the Ox, and whenever it came near attempted to bite it. At last the Ox had to give up the hope of getting at the straw, and went away muttering :

"Ah, people often grudge others what they cannot enjoy themselves."

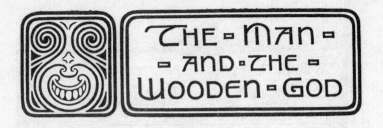

THE·MAN·
·AND·THE·
WOODEN·GOD

I N the old days men used to worship stocks and stones and idols, and prayed to

them to give them luck. It happened that
a Man had often prayed to a wooden idol
he had received from his father, but his luck
never seemed to change. He prayed and he
prayed, but still he remained as unlucky as
ever. One day in the greatest rage he went
to the Wooden God, and with one blow
swept it down from its pedestal. The idol

broke in two, and what did he see? An
immense number of coins flying all over
the place.

The FISHER

 A FISHER once took his bagpipes to the bank of a river, and played upon them with the hope of making the fish rise; but never a one put his nose out of the water. So he cast his net into the river and soon drew it forth filled with fish. Then he took his bagpipes again, and, as he played, the fish leapt up in the net. "Ah, you dance now when I play," said he.

"Yes," said an old Fish:

"𝔚𝔥𝔢𝔫 𝔶𝔬𝔲 𝔞𝔯𝔢 𝔦𝔫 𝔞 𝔪𝔞𝔫'𝔰 𝔭𝔬𝔴𝔢𝔯 𝔶𝔬𝔲 𝔪𝔲𝔰𝔱 𝔡𝔬
𝔞𝔰 𝔥𝔢 𝔟𝔦𝔡𝔰 𝔶𝔬𝔲."

The Shepherd's Boy.

THERE was once a young Shepherd Boy who tended his sheep at the foot of a mountain near a dark forest. It was rather lonely for him all day, so he thought upon a plan by which he could get a little company and some excitement. He rushed down towards the village calling out "Wolf, Wolf," and the villagers came out to meet him, and some of them stopped with him for a considerable time. This pleased the boy so much that a few days afterwards he tried the same trick, and again the villagers came to his help. But shortly after this a Wolf actually did come out from the forest, and began to worry the sheep, and the boy of course cried out "Wolf,

Wolf," still louder than before. But this
time the villagers, who had been fooled twice
before, thought the boy was again deceiving
them, and nobody stirred to come to his help.
So the Wolf made a good meal off the boy's
flock, and when the boy complained, the wise
man of the village said :

"A liar will not be believed, even when
he speaks the truth."

THE
YOUNG
THIEF
AND
HIS
MOTHER

A YOUNG man had been caught in a daring act of theft and had been condemned to be executed for it. He expressed his desire to see his Mother, and to speak with her before he was led to execution, and of course this was granted. When his Mother came to him he said : "I want to whisper to you," and when she brought her ear near him, he nearly bit it off. All the bystanders were horrified, and asked him what he could mean by such brutal and inhuman conduct. "It is to punish her," he said. "When I was young I began with stealing little things, and brought them home to Mother. Instead of rebuking and punishing me, she laughed and said : 'It will not be noticed.' It is because of her that I am here to-day."

"He is right, woman," said the Priest ; "the Lord hath said :

"𝕿rain up a child in the way he should go ; and when he is old he will not depart therefrom."

THE MAN & HIS TWO WIVES

IN the old days, when men were allowed to have many wives, a middle-aged Man had one wife that was old and one that was young; each loved him very much, and desired to see him like herself. Now the Man's hair was turning grey, which the young Wife did not like, as it made him look too old for her husband. So every night she used to comb his hair and pick out the white ones. But the elder Wife saw her husband growing grey with great pleasure, for she did not like to be mistaken for his mother. So every morning she used to arrange his hair and pick out as many of

the black ones as she could. The consequence
was the Man soon found himself entirely bald.

𝔜ield to all and you will soon have nothing
to yield.

The·Nurse·&·the Wolf

"BE quiet now," said an old Nurse to a child sitting on her lap. "If you make that noise again I will throw you to the Wolf." Now it chanced that a Wolf was passing close under the window as this was said. So he crouched down by the side of the house and waited. "I am in good luck to-day," thought he. "It is sure to cry soon, and a daintier morsel I haven't had for many a long day." So he waited, and he waited, and he waited, till at last the child began to cry, and the Wolf came forward before the window, and looked up to the Nurse, wagging his tail. But all the Nurse did was to shut down the window and call for help, and the dogs of the house came rushing out. "Ah," said the Wolf as he galloped away,

"Enemies' promises were made to be broken."

 TORTOISE desired to change its place of residence, so he asked an Eagle to carry him to his new home, promising her a rich reward for her trouble. The Eagle agreed, and seizing the Tortoise by the shell with her talons, soared aloft. On their way they met a Crow, who said to the Eagle: "Tortoise is good eating." "The shell is too hard," said the Eagle in reply. "The rocks will soon crack the shell," was the Crow's answer; and the Eagle, taking the hint, let fall the Tortoise on a sharp rock, and the two birds made a hearty meal off the Tortoise.

𝔑𝔢𝔳𝔢𝔯 𝔰𝔬𝔞𝔯 𝔞𝔩𝔬𝔣𝔱 𝔬𝔫 𝔞𝔫 𝔢𝔫𝔢𝔪𝔶'𝔰 𝔭𝔦𝔫𝔦𝔬𝔫𝔰.

The Two Birds made a hearty meal off the Tortoise.

 fine day two Crabs came out from their home to take a stroll on the sand. "Child," said the mother, "you are walking very ungracefully. You should accustom yourself to walking straight forward without twisting from side to side."

"Pray, mother," said the young one, "do but set the example yourself, and I will follow you."

Example is the best precept.

The Aſs in the Lion's Skin.

AN Ass once found a Lion's skin which the hunters had left out in the sun to dry. He put it on and went towards his native village. All fled at his approach, both men and animals, and he was a proud Ass that day. In his delight he lifted up his voice and brayed, but then every one knew him, and his owner came up and gave him a sound cudgelling for the fright he had caused. And shortly afterwards a Fox came up to him and said: "Ah, I knew you by your voice."

Fine clothes may disguise, but silly words will disclose a fool.

"I · knew · you · by · your · voice!"

the Two Fellows and the Bear.

TWO Fellows were travelling together through a wood, when a Bear rushed out upon them. One of the travellers happened to be in front, and he seized hold of the branch of a tree, and hid himself among the leaves. The other, seeing no help for it, threw himself flat down upon the ground, with his face in the dust. The Bear, coming up to him, put his muzzle close to his ear, and sniffed and sniffed. But at last with a growl he shook his head and slouched off, for bears will not touch dead meat. Then the fellow in the tree came down

to his comrade, and, laughing, said : " What
was it that Master Bruin whispered to you ? "
" He told me," said the other,

" 𝔑𝔢𝔳𝔢𝔯 𝔱𝔯𝔲𝔰𝔱 𝔞 𝔣𝔯𝔦𝔢𝔫𝔡 𝔴𝔥𝔬 𝔡𝔢𝔰𝔢𝔯𝔱𝔰 𝔶𝔬𝔲
𝔞𝔱 𝔞 𝔭𝔦𝔫𝔠𝔥."

THE TWO POTS

TWO Pots had been left on the bank of a river, one of brass, and one of earthenware. When the tide rose they both floated off down the stream. Now the earthenware pot tried its best to keep aloof from the brass one, which cried out : "Fear nothing, friend, I will not strike you."

"But I may come in contact with you," said the other, "if I come too close ; and whether I hit you, or you hit me, I shall suffer for it."

The strong and the weak cannot keep company.

THE FOUR OXEN & THE LION

A LION used to prowl about a field in which Four Oxen used to dwell. Many a time he tried to attack them; but whenever he came near they turned their tails to one another, so that whichever way he approached them he was met by the horns of one of them. At last, however, they fell a-quarrelling among themselves, and each went off to pasture alone in a separate corner of the field. Then the Lion attacked them one by one and soon made an end of all four.

United we stand, divided we fall.

THE FISHER & THE LITTLE FISH

IT happened that a fisher, after fishing all day, caught only a little fish. "Pray, let me go, master," said the Fish. "I am much too small for your eating just now. If you put me back into the river I shall soon grow, then you can make a fine meal off me."

"Nay, nay, my little Fish," said the Fisher, "I have you now. I may not catch you hereafter."

A little thing in hand is worth more than a great thing in prospect.

Avaricious and Envious

TWO neighbours came before Jupiter and prayed him to grant their hearts' desire. Now the one was full of avarice, and the other eaten up with envy. So to punish them both, Jupiter granted that each might have whatever he wished for himself, but only on condition that his neighbour had twice as much. The Avaricious man prayed to have a room full of gold. No sooner said than done; but all his joy was turned to grief when he found that his neighbour had two rooms full of the precious metal. Then came the turn of the Envious man, who could not bear to think that his neighbour had any joy at all. So he prayed that he might have one of his own eyes put out, by which means his companion would become totally blind.

Vices are their own punishment.

THE CROW & THE PITCHER

CROW, half-dead with thirst, came upon a Pitcher which had once been full of water; but when the Crow put its beak into the mouth of the Pitcher he found that only very little water was left in it, and that he could not reach far enough down to get at it. He tried, and he tried, but at last had to give up in despair. Then a thought came to him, and he took a pebble and dropped it into the Pitcher. Then he took another pebble and dropped it into the Pitcher. Then he took another pebble and dropped that into the Pitcher. Then he took another pebble and dropped that into the Pitcher. Then he took another pebble and dropped that into the Pitcher. Then he took another pebble and dropped that into the Pitcher. At last, at last, he saw the water mount up near him; and after casting in a few more pebbles he was able to quench his thirst and save his life.

Little by little does the trick.

The Man & the Satyr

A MAN had lost his way in a wood one bitter winter's night. As he was roaming about, a Satyr came up to him, and finding that he had lost his way, promised to give him a lodging for the night, and guide him out of the forest in the morning. As he went along to the Satyr's cell, the Man raised both his hands to his mouth and kept on blowing at them. "What do you do that for?" said the Satyr.

"My hands are numb with the cold," said the Man, "and my breath warms them."

After this they arrived at the Satyr's home, and soon the Satyr put a smoking dish of porridge before him. But when the Man raised his spoon to his mouth he began blowing upon it. "And what do you do that for?" said the Satyr.

"The porridge is too hot, and my breath will cool it."

"Out you go," said the Satyr. "I will have nought to do with a man who can blow hot and cold with the same breath."

THE GOOSE WITH THE GOLDEN EGGS

ONE day a countryman going to the nest of his Goose found there an egg all yellow and glittering.

When he took it up it was as heavy as lead and he was going to throw it away, because he thought a trick had been played upon him. But he took it home on second thoughts, and soon found to his delight that it was an egg of pure gold. Every morning the same thing occurred, and he soon became rich by selling his eggs. As he grew rich he grew greedy; and thinking to get at once all the gold the Goose could give, he killed it and opened it only to find, —nothing.

Greed oft o'erreaches itself.

:Greed·to·Need·doth·surely·lead:

:THE: :GOOSE: :WITH: :THE: :GOLDEN: :EGGS:

The · Labourer · and the Nightingale

LABOURER lay listening to a Nightingale's song throughout the summer night. So pleased was he with it that the next night he set a trap for it and captured it. "Now that I have caught thee," he cried, "thou shalt always sing to me."

"We Nightingales never sing in a cage," said the bird.

"Then I'll eat thee," said the Labourer. "I have always heard say that nightingale on toast is a dainty morsel."

"Nay, kill me not," said the Nightingale; "but let me free, and I'll tell thee three things far better worth than my poor body." The Labourer let him loose, and he flew up to a

branch of a tree and said : "Never believe a
captive's promise ; that's one thing. Then
again : Keep what you have. And a third
piece of advice is : Sorrow not over what is
lost forever." Then the song-bird flew away.

The Fox the Cock and the Dog.

ONE moonlight night a Fox was prowling about a farmer's hen-coop, and saw a Cock roosting high up beyond his reach. "Good news, good news!" he cried.

"Why, what is that?" said the Cock.

"King Lion has declared a universal truce. No beast may hurt a bird henceforth, but all shall dwell together in brotherly friendship."

"Why, that is good news," said the Cock; "and there I see some one coming, with whom we can share the good tidings." And so saying he craned his neck forward and looked afar off.

"What is it you see?" said the Fox.

"It is only my master's Dog that is coming towards us. What, going so soon?" he continued, as the Fox began to turn away as soon as he had heard the news. "Will you not stop and congratulate the Dog on the reign of universal peace?"

"I would gladly do so," said the Fox, "but I fear he may not have heard of King Lion's decree."

Cunning often outwits itself.

"What, going so soon?"

HE Wind and the Sun were disputing which was the stronger. Suddenly they saw a traveller coming down the road, and the Sun said: "I see a way to decide our dispute. Whichever of us can cause that traveller to take off his cloak

shall be regarded as the stronger. You begin." So the Sun retired behind a cloud, and the Wind began to blow as hard as it could upon the traveller. But the harder he blew the more closely did the traveller wrap his cloak round him, till at last the Wind had to give up in despair. Then the Sun came out and shone in all his glory upon the traveller, who soon found it too hot to walk with his cloak on.

Kindness effects more than Severity.

HERCULES
AND THE
WAGGONER

A WAGGONER was once driving a heavy load along a very muddy way. At last he came to a part of the road where the wheels sank halfway into the mire, and the more the horses pulled, the deeper sank the wheels. So the Waggoner threw down his whip, and knelt down and prayed to Hercules the Strong. "O Hercules, help me in this my hour of distress," quoth he. But Hercules appeared to him, and said :

"Tut, man, don't sprawl there. Get up and put your shoulder to the wheel."

𝕿𝖍𝖊 𝖌𝖔𝖉𝖘 𝖍𝖊𝖑𝖕 𝖙𝖍𝖊𝖒 𝖙𝖍𝖆𝖙 𝖍𝖊𝖑𝖕 𝖙𝖍𝖊𝖒𝖘𝖊𝖑𝖛𝖊𝖘.

ONCE upon a time there was a Miser who used to hide his gold at the foot of a tree in his garden; but every week he used to go and dig it up and gloat over his gains. A robber, who had noticed this, went and dug up the gold and decamped with it. When the Miser next came to gloat over his treasures, he found nothing but the empty hole. He tore his hair, and raised such an outcry that all the neighbours came around him, and he told them how he used to come and visit his gold. "Did you ever take any of it out?" asked one of them.

"Nay," said he, "I only came to look at it."

"Then come again and look at the hole," said a neighbour; "it will do you just as much good."

Wealth unused might as well not exist.

THE MAN THE BOY & THE DONKEY.

 MAN and his son were once going with their Donkey to market. As they were walking along by its side a countryman passed them and said: "You fools, what is a Donkey for but to ride upon?"

So the Man put the Boy on the Donkey and they went on their way. But soon they passed a group of men, one of whom said: "See that lazy youngster, he lets his father walk while he rides."

So the Man ordered his Boy to get off, and got on himself. But they hadn't gone far when they passed two women, one of whom said to the other: "Shame on that lazy lout to let his poor little son trudge along."

Well the Man didn't know what to

do, but at last he took his Boy up
before him on the Donkey. By this time
they had come to the town, and the passers-
by began to jeer and point at them. The
Man stopped and asked what they were
scoffing at The men said : "Aren't you
ashamed of yourself for overloading that poor
Donkey of yours—you and your hulking son ?"

The Man and Boy got off and tried to think
what to do. They thought and they thought,
till at last they cut down a pole, tied the
Donkey's feet to it, and raised the pole and
the Donkey to their shoulders. They went
along amid the laughter of all who met them

till they came to Market Bridge, when the Donkey, getting one of his feet loose, kicked out and caused the Boy to drop his end of the pole. In the struggle the Donkey fell over the bridge, and his fore-feet being tied together he was drowned.

"That will teach you," said an old man who had followed them:

"𝔓lease all, and you will please none."

A FOX after crossing a river got its tail entangled in a bush, and could not move. A number of Mosquitoes seeing its plight settled upon it and enjoyed a good meal undisturbed by its tail. A hedgehog strolling by took pity upon the Fox and went up to him: "You are in a bad way, neighbour," said the hedgehog; "shall I relieve you by driving off those Mosquitoes who are sucking your blood?"

"Thank you, Master Hedgehog," said the Fox, "but I would rather not."

"Why, how is that?" asked the hedgehog.

"Well, you see," was the answer, "these Mosquitoes have had their fill; if you drive these away, others will come with fresh appetite and bleed me to death."

The Fox without a tail :.

IT happened that a Fox caught its tail
in a trap, and in struggling to release
himself lost all of it but the stump.
At first he was ashamed to show
himself among his fellow foxes. But at last
he determined to put a bolder face upon his
misfortune, and summoned all the foxes to a
general meeting to consider a proposal which
he had to place before them. When they
had assembled together the Fox proposed that
they should all do away with their tails. He
pointed out how inconvenient a tail was when
they were pursued by their enemies, the dogs;
how much it was in the way when they

desired to sit down and hold a friendly
conversation with one another. He failed to
see any advantage in carrying about such a
useless encumbrance. "That is all very
well," said one of the older foxes ; "but I do
not think you would have recommended us
to dispense with our chief ornament if you
had not happened to lose it yourself."

Distrust interested advice.

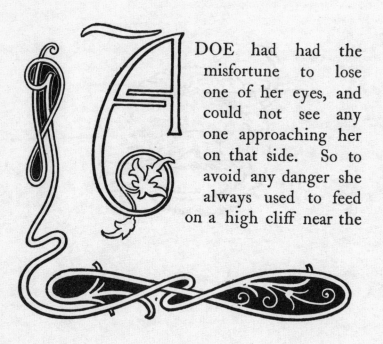

A DOE had had the misfortune to lose one of her eyes, and could not see any one approaching her on that side. So to avoid any danger she always used to feed on a high cliff near the sea, with her sound eye looking towards the land. By this means she could see whenever the hunters approached her on land, and often escaped by this means. But the hunters found out that she was blind of one eye, and hiring a boat rowed under the cliff where she used to feed and shot her from the sea. " Ah," cried she with her dying voice,

"𝔜ou cannot escape your fate."

BELLING
THE
CAT

LONG ago, the mice held a general council to consider what measures they could take to outwit their common enemy, the Cat. Some said this, and some said that; but at last a young mouse got up and said he had a proposal to make, which he thought would meet the case. "You will all agree," said he, "that our chief danger consists in the sly and treacherous manner in which the enemy approaches us. Now, if we could receive some signal of her approach, we could easily escape from her. I venture, therefore, to propose that a small bell be procured, and attached by a ribbon round the neck of the Cat. By this means we should always know when she was about, and could easily retire while she was in the neighbourhood."

This proposal met with general applause, until an old mouse got up and said : "That is all very well, but who is to bell the Cat?" The mice looked at one another and nobody spoke. Then the old mouse said :

"𝔍𝔱 𝔦𝔰 𝔢𝔞𝔰𝔶 𝔱𝔬 𝔭𝔯𝔬𝔭𝔬𝔰𝔢 𝔦𝔪𝔭𝔬𝔰𝔰𝔦𝔟𝔩𝔢 𝔯𝔢𝔪𝔢𝔡𝔦𝔢𝔰."

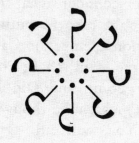

"That is all
very well,
But
WHO
IS
to
the Cat.

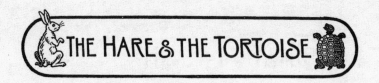

THE HARE & THE TORTOISE

THE Hare was once boasting of his speed before the other animals. "I have never yet been beaten," said he, "when I put forth my full speed. I challenge any one here to race with me."

The Tortoise said quietly : "I accept your challenge."

"That is a good joke," said the Hare; "I could dance round you all the way."

"Keep your boasting till you've beaten," answered the Tortoise. "Shall we race?"

So a course was fixed and a start was made. The Hare darted almost out of sight at once, but soon stopped and, to show his contempt for the Tortoise, lay down to have a nap.

The Tortoise plodded on and plodded on, and
when the Hare awoke from his nap, he saw
the Tortoise just near the winning-post and
could not run up in time to save the race.
Then said the Tortoise :

"𝔓𝔩𝔬𝔡𝔡𝔦𝔫𝔤 𝔴𝔦𝔫𝔰 𝔱𝔥𝔢 𝔯𝔞𝔠𝔢."

The Old Man and Death

AN old labourer, bent double with age and toil, was gathering sticks in a forest. At last he grew so tired and hopeless that he threw down the bundle of sticks, and cried out : " I cannot bear this life any longer. Ah, I wish Death would only come and take me ! "

As he spoke, Death, a grisly skeleton,

appeared and said to him : " What wouldst thou, Mortal ? I heard thee call me."

" Please, sir," replied the woodcutter, " would you kindly help me to lift this faggot of sticks on to my shoulder?"

We would often be sorry if our wishes were gratified.

The Hare with many friends

A HARE was very popular with the other beasts who all claimed to be her friends. But one day she heard the hounds approaching and hoped to escape them by the aid of her many Friends. So she went to the horse, and asked him to carry her away from the hounds on his back. But he declined, stating that he had important work to do for his master. "He felt sure," he said, "that all her other friends would come to her assistance." She then applied to the bull, and hoped that he would repel the hounds with his horns. The bull replied: "I am very sorry, but I have an appointment with a lady; but I feel sure that our friend the goat will do what you want." The goat, however, feared that his back might do her some harm if he took her upon it. The ram, he felt sure, was the

proper friend to apply to. So she went to
the ram and told him the case. The ram
replied : " Another time, my dear friend. I
do not like to interfere on the present occasion,
as hounds have been known to eat sheep as
well as hares." The Hare then applied, as
a last hope, to the calf, who regretted that he
was unable to help her, as he did not like to
take the responsibility upon himself, as so
many older persons than himself had declined
the task. By this time the hounds were quite
near, and the Hare took to her heels and
luckily escaped.

𝔥𝔢 𝔱𝔥𝔞𝔱 𝔥𝔞𝔰 𝔪𝔞𝔫𝔶 𝔣𝔯𝔦𝔢𝔫𝔡𝔰, 𝔥𝔞𝔰 𝔫𝔬 𝔣𝔯𝔦𝔢𝔫𝔡𝔰.

THE LION IN LOVE

LION once fell in love with a
beautiful maiden and proposed
marriage to her parents. The old
people did not know what to say.
They did not like to give their daughter to
the Lion, yet they did not wish to enrage the
King of Beasts. At last the father said : "We
feel highly honoured by your Majesty's
proposal, but you see our daughter is a tender
young thing, and we fear that in the
vehemence of your affection you might
possibly do her some injury. Might I
venture to suggest that your Majesty should
have your claws removed, and your teeth
extracted, then we would gladly consider
your proposal again." The Lion was so
much in love that he had his claws trimmed
and his big teeth taken out. But when he

came again to the parents of the young girl
they simply laughed in his face, and bade him
do his worst.

Love can tame the wildest.

UNITY · IS · STRENGTH

The Bundle of Sticks

AN old man on the point of death summoned his sons around him to give them some parting advice. He ordered his servants to bring in a faggot of sticks, and said to his eldest son : "Break it." The son strained and strained, but with all his efforts was unable to break the Bundle. The other sons also tried, but none of them was successful. "Untie the faggots," said the father, "and each of you take a stick." When they had done so, he called out to them : "Now, break," and each stick was easily broken. "You see my meaning," said their father.

"Union gives strength."

The Lion, the Fox and the Beasts

THE Lion once gave out that he was sick unto death, and summoned the animals to come and hear his last Will and Testament. So the Goat came to the Lion's cave, and stopped there listening for a long time. Then a Sheep went in, and before she came out a Calf came up to receive the last wishes of the Lord of the Beasts. But soon the Lion seemed to recover, and came to the mouth of his cave, and saw the Fox who had been waiting outside for some time. "Why do you not come to pay your respects to me?" said the Lion to the Fox.

"I beg your Majesty's pardon," said the Fox, "but I noticed the track of the animals that have already come to you; and while I see many hoof-marks going in, I see none coming out. Till the animals that have entered your cave come out again I prefer to remain in the open air."

It is easier to get into the enemy's toils than out again.

The Ass's Brains

THE Lion and the Fox went hunting together. The Lion, on the advice of the Fox, sent a message to the Ass, proposing to make an alliance between their two families. The Ass came to the place of meeting, overjoyed at the prospect of a royal alliance. But when he came there the Lion simply pounced on the Ass, and said to the Fox : "Here is our dinner for to-day. Watch you here while I go and have a nap. Woe betide you if you touch my prey." The Lion went away and the Fox waited ; but finding that his master did not return, ventured to take out the brains of the Ass and ate them up. When the Lion came back he soon noticed the absence of the brains, and asked the Fox in a terrible voice : "What have you done with the brains ?"

"Brains, your Majesty ! it had none, or it would never have fallen into your trap."

Wit has always an answer ready.

The Eagle & the Arrow

AN Eagle was soaring through the air when suddenly it heard the whizz of an Arrow, and felt itself wounded to death. Slowly it fluttered down to the earth, with its life-blood pouring out of it. Looking down upon the Arrow with which it had been pierced, it found that the haft of the Arrow had been feathered with one of its own plumes. "Alas!" it cried, as it died,

"We often give our enemies the means for our own destruction."

THE CAT-MAIDEN

THE gods were once disputing whether it was possible for a living being to change its nature. Jupiter said "Yes," but Venus said "No." So, to try the question, Jupiter turned a Cat into a Maiden, and gave her to a young man for wife. The wedding was duly performed and the young couple sat down to the wedding-feast. "See," said Jupiter to Venus, "how becomingly she behaves. Who could tell that yesterday she was but a Cat? Surely her nature is changed?"

"Wait a minute," replied Venus, and let loose a mouse into the room. No sooner did

the bride see this than she jumped up from her
seat and tried to pounce upon the mouse. "Ah,
you see," said Venus,

"𝔑ature will out."

The Milkmaid
and her Pail

PATTY, the Milkmaid, was going to market carrying her milk in a Pail on her head. As she went along she began calculating what she would do with the money she would get for the milk. "I'll buy some fowls from Farmer Brown," said she, "and they will lay eggs each morning, which I will sell to the parson's wife. With the money that I get from the sale of these eggs I'll buy myself a new dimity frock and a chip hat; and when I go to market, won't all the young men come up and speak to me! Polly Shaw will be that jealous; but I don't care. I shall just look at her and toss my head like this." As she spoke, she tossed her head back, the Pail fell off it and all the milk was spilt. So she had to go home and tell her mother what had occurred.

"Ah, my child," said her mother,

"Do not count your chickens before they are hatched."

The Horse & the Ass

A HORSE and an Ass were travelling together, the Horse prancing along in its fine trappings, the Ass carrying with difficulty the heavy weight in its panniers. "I wish I were you," sighed the Ass; "nothing to do and well fed, and all that fine harness upon you." Next day, however, there was a great battle, and the Horse was wounded to death in the final charge of the day. His friend, the Ass, happened to pass by shortly afterwards and found him on the point of death. "I was wrong," said the Ass :

"𝕭etter humble security than gilded danger."

The·Trumpeter taken·Prisoner.

 TRUMPETER during a battle ventured too near the enemy and was captured by them. They were about to proceed to put him to death when he begged them to hear his plea for mercy. "I do not fight," said he, "and indeed carry no weapon; I only blow this trumpet, and surely that cannot harm you; then why should you kill me?"

"You may not fight yourself," said the others, "but you encourage and guide your men to the fight."

Words may be deeds.

" You fools ! see what you have been hissing."

The Buffoon &
the Countryman

AT a country fair there was a Buffoon who made all the people laugh by imitating the cries of various animals. He finished off by squeaking so like a pig that the spectators thought that he had a porker concealed about him. But a Countryman who stood by said : "Call that a pig's squeak! Nothing like it. You give me till to-morrow and I will show you what it's like." The audience laughed, but next day, sure enough, the Countryman appeared on the stage, and putting his head down squealed so hideously that the spectators hissed and threw stones at him to make him stop. "You fools!" he cried, "see what you have been hissing," and held up a little pig whose ear he had been pinching to make him utter the squeals.

Men often applaud an imitation, and hiss the real thing.

The Old Woman and the Wine-Jar

YOU must know that sometimes old women like a glass of wine. One of this sort once found a Wine-jar lying in the road, and eagerly went up to it hoping to find it full. But when she took it up she found that all the wine had been drunk out of it. Still she took a long sniff at the mouth of the Jar. "Ah," she cried,

"What memories cling round the instruments of our pleasure."

The Fox & the Goat

BY an unlucky chance a Fox fell into a deep well from which he could not get out. A Goat passed by shortly afterwards, and asked the Fox what he was doing down there. "Oh, have you not heard?" said the Fox; "there is going to be a great drought, so I jumped down here in order to be sure to have water by me. Why don't you come down too?" The Goat thought well of this advice, and jumped down into the well. But the Fox immediately jumped on her back, and by putting his foot on her long horns managed to jump up to the edge of the well. "Good-bye, friend," said the Fox; "remember next time,

"Never trust the advice of a man in difficulties."

And this is the end of Æsop's Fables
HURRAH !

The End

So the tales were told ages before Æsop; and asses under lions' manes roared in Hebrew; and sly foxes flattered in Etruscan; and wolves in sheep's clothing gnashed their teeth in Sanskrit, no doubt.

THACKERAY, *The Newcomes.*